This Little Tiger book belongs to:

_____

_____

_____

For Holly, with love ~ K W

To my beloved Grand-Maman.
Click, Clack, Croc' Geneviève! ~ J D

LITTLE TIGER PRESS
1 The Coda Centre, 189 Munster Road, London SW6 6AW
www.littletiger.co.uk

First published in Great Britain 2009
This edition published 2010

Text copyright © Kathryn White 2009
Illustrations copyright © Joëlle Dreidemy 2009
Kathryn White and Joëlle Dreidemy have asserted their rights
to be identified as the author and illustrator of this work under
the Copyright, Designs and Patents Act, 1988

A CIP catalogue record for this book is available from
the British Library

All rights reserved · ISBN 978-1-84506-978-0

Printed in China · LTP/1400/0644/0413

10 9 8 7 6 5 4 3 2

Click Clack Crocodile's Back

Kathryn White

Joëlle Dreidemy

LITTLE TIGER PRESS

London

Tremble with fear, Crocodile's near.
He's sneaking by, with a glint in his eye,
Slyly disguised as the trunk of a tree,
Ready to **snatch** you and **eat** you for tea!

Slip,
slap,

it's Crocodile's trap.

He's **squelching**
and **sliding**

in mud, where he's hiding . . .

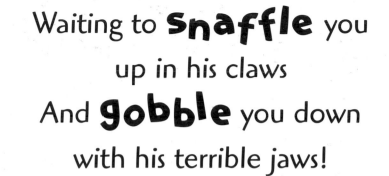

Waiting to **snaffle** you
up in his claws
And **gobble** you down
with his terrible jaws!

WATCH OUT,
Crocodile's about!
Flamingos are **Preening**
then one of them spies,

Down in the rushes,
two **mean,**
greedy eyes . . .

"LOOK OUT, IT'S CROCODILE!"

everyone cries.

"He keeps **creeping** up on me," Elephant groans. "That **big, sneaky** Crocodile," everyone moans.

But Monkey is cool,
Monkey is clever –
He has a plan they can
all do together.

So brave little Monkey
swings down to the river.

"A gift for Crocodile,"
he says with a shiver.

"A **gift**?" says Crocodile,
very unsure.
"Why . . . I've never been
given a **gift** before."

Monkey holds out his **trembling** hand.
"This present will make you look
wonderfully grand.
It's a jacket I made from banana peel."

Crocodile grins
and says,
"Simply ideal!"

"We've made you a hat!" the flamingos flock in,
Making a **mess** and a terrible **din**.

And Crocodile roars,
"Oh, won't I look great?
I'll be **dashing** and **sporty**
and so **up-to-date!**"

Then Elephant trumped,
"Here's some jewellery as well.
It **jingles** and **jangles**
and **chimes** like a bell."

"OH WOW,"

says Crocodile.
"How splendid I'll be,
When I **sneak** and I **creep**
and I **hunt** for my tea."

"And won't you look **fabulous**," everyone cheers,

"When you wear these new coconut charms on your ears?"

"Awesome!" says Crocodile,
giving a

grrrowl,

"I'll wear them each time
I go out on the **prowl**."

So Crocodile grinned
and his **greedy** eyes shone,
As he shot off to try
all his new presents on.

Shhhhh!

Listen – what's
making that sound?

It's **jingling**
and **jangling** and
prowling around.

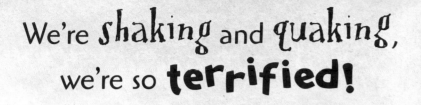

We're **shaking** and **quaking**,
we're so **terrified!**

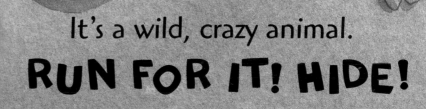

It's a wild, crazy animal.
RUN FOR IT! HIDE!

TEE
HEE!

HA
HA!

HO
HO!

Click, clack, Crocodile's back!

In his necklace and jacket, and earrings and hat.

He looks just **fantastic,**

but he's **cross** as can be.

For everyone's hiding – and he can't catch his tea!

Make a noise with these Little Tiger Press books!

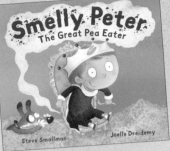

Smelly Peter
The Great Pea Eater
Steve Smallman · Joelle Dreidemy

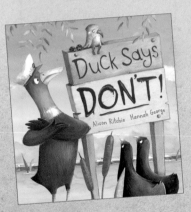

Duck Says DON'T!
Alison Ritchie · Hannah George

with fold-out pages

MY MONSTER DUMPER TRUCK
Steve Smallman · Joelle Dreidemy

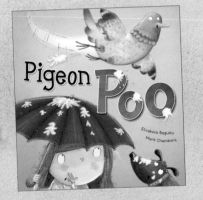

Pigeon POO
Elizabeth Baguley · Mark Chambers

When Will It Snow?
Kathryn White · Alison Edgson

Paul Bright · Michael Terry

CRUNCH MUNCH DINOSAUR LUNCH!

For information regarding any of the above
titles or for our catalogue, please contact us:
Little Tiger Press, 1 The Coda Centre,
189 Munster Road, London SW6 6AW
Tel: 020 7385 6333 · Fax: 020 7385 7333
E-mail: info@littletiger.co.uk · www.littletiger.co.uk